GREAT JOY

The week before Christmas, a monkey appeared on the corner of
Fifth and Vine. He was wearing a green vest and a red hat, and with him
was a man, an organ grinder, who played music for the people on the street.

In the daytime, when the sun shone, the sequins on the monkey's vest glittered and flashed, and from the window of her apartment, Frances could see the tin cup he held out to the people who walked by.

Sometimes, if it was very quiet for just a minute, she could hear the music. It came across the crowded sidewalk and up through the windows, and even though the organ grinder and the monkey were just across the street, the songs sounded sad and far away, like the music from a dream.

"Where do they go at night?" Frances asked.

"Who?" said her mother.

"That man and his monkey."

"Oh, Frances," said her mother. "Don't ask me questions that I can't answer. I'm sure they go somewhere. Everyone goes somewhere."

"But where?" said Frances.

"I have no idea," said her mother. "Turn around."

Frances turned.

Her mother pinned the bottom of her robe.

"There," said her mother. "Now all I have to do is hem it, and you'll be ready. Have you memorized your line?"

"Yes," said Frances.

"Are you excited about the pageant?"

"Yes," said Frances. And she turned away from her mother and looked out the window at the monkey.

That night, Frances made herself stay awake. She hummed songs and said her multiplication tables. She named the capitals of each state—St. Paul, Tallahassee, Harrisburg—one after the other. Every time she felt as if she might fall asleep, she shook her head and pinched her arm and opened her eyes wide.

Finally, at midnight, Frances got out of bed and crept down the hallway to the living room.

She looked down into the street. She saw the organ grinder, but where was the monkey? Her heart thumped. And then she saw him, tucked inside the man's overcoat, his small red hat still on his head.

"Look at me," Frances whispered. "Look up here."

It was the organ grinder who looked up.

He took his cap from his head and raised it to her.

"They sleep on the street," Frances said the next morning, "even when it snows."

"Oh, Frances," said her mother.

"Maybe they could come for dinner?"

"No, they can't come for dinner," said her mother.

"Why not?"

"They're strangers, that's why. Eat your breakfast, Frances. You've got a big day ahead of you."

All that day it snowed. But by evening, in time for the pageant, the sky cleared. The snow was so deep that Frances had to wear her boots for the walk to the church.

The organ grinder and the monkey were still on their corner.

Frances ran up and put a nickel in the monkey's cup. "I'm going to be in the Christmas play tonight," she said. "I get to wear wings, and I have one line to say. Do you want to hear it?"

"Frances," her mother said, "we're going to be late. Let's go."

"You can come," Frances said, turning back. "The play is at the church. It's just down the street. You can both come."

The organ grinder smiled at her. But his eyes looked sad.

At the church, everyone else was already in costume. "Hurry," the choir director said as he helped Frances put on her wings.

The shepherds walked out first, and then the choir director pointed to Frances. "Now," he whispered.

Frances stood very still. She opened her mouth, but the words would not come.

"Say it," whispered one of the shepherds.

"Say it," hissed an angel who did not have any lines of her own.

The camel, which was really two people, swayed nervously back and forth.

But Frances could not speak. All she could think about was how cold it was outside and how sad the organ grinder's eyes were, even when he smiled.

The world was quiet.
Everyone waited.

Then, at the back
of the sanctuary,
a door opened.

Frances smiled.

"Behold!"

she shouted.

"I bring you tidings of Great Joy!"

And because the words felt so right,

Frances said them again.

"Great Joy."

*With great gratitude for open doors and for all the people
who have welcomed me in*
K. D.

To Yana Yelina with love
B. I.

Text copyright © 2007 by Kate DiCamillo
Illustrations copyright © 2007 by Bagram Ibatoulline

First edition in this format 2010

Library of Congress Cataloging-in-Publication Data is available.

Library of Congress Catalog Card Number 2007029934

ISBN 978-0-7636-4996-8 (midi hardcover)

10 11 12 13 14 15 16 SCP 10 9 8 7 6 5 4 3 2 1

Printed in Humen, Dongguan, China

This book was typeset in ITC Golden Cockerel.
The illustrations were done in acrylic gouache.

Candlewick Press
99 Dover Street
Somerville, Massachusetts 02144

visit us at www.candlewick.com